Idrian N. Resnick

FIREMAN MIKE

A Novella

ADDITIONAL BOOKS BY IDRIAN N. RESNICK

Fiction

The Invisible Hand
The Bell
Light Shorts

Non-Fiction

The Handbook of Africa
Tanzania: Revolution by Education
The Long Transition: Building Socialism in Tanzania
A Guide for the Use and Control of Consultants
by Native Americans
Foreign Trade and Payments in Tanzania
Instructor's Guide to the IBFAN Monitoring Protocol
Humpty-Dumpty Sister

Idrian N. Resnick

FIREMAN MIKE

A novella

Fireman Mike

ISBN: 978-1507656297
ISBN-10: 1507656297
Library of Congress Control Number: 2015903258
CreateSpace Independent Publishing Platform, North Charleston, SC

Printed in the United States of America

To my grandson, Logan

ACKNOWLEDGEMENTS

I am indebted to Susan Wegener, who copy-edited the manuscript and was my "grammar maven."

"…into the wild blue yonder,
Climbing high into the sun;
…down in flame."

US Army Air Corps Song

Chapter 1

My daddy is lost. He died way up in the sky and no one ever saw him again. I want to go way high and find him. My mom and sister say I can't but I know I can.

I remember when our train came in from New Jersey, coal soot blowing in the open windows, and the prickly blue seat scratching me everywhere. I was sticky hot and the air in front of New York was all wiggly.

"There it is, Mom!" my big sister, Susan, squealed. "There's New York! Oh, God! I can't believe it. They're waiting for me, I just know it."

At first the skyscrapers looked like little toy buildings you'd put around an electric train set. A lot stuck way up above the rest.

"Close your mouth, Tommy," my mother said. "You'll get sick on the coal dust."

"Why won't he get sick breathing through his nose?" Susan asked.

"Because there are little hairs in his nose that catch a lot of it."

"What?" I cried. "I don't have hairs in my nose." I wiped and rubbed.

1

"Is that why my boogers have been black since we got on the train?" Susan wanted to know.

"Exactly."

"Look, there!" I yelled. "What's that building? And that one like a needle with the sun on it?"

"The big one is the Empire State Building." Mom's voice sounded real serious. "The tallest building in the world."

"Gosh!"

"God!"

"The other one's the Chrysler building, after the car company."

"Is that the tallest second building in the world?" I asked. "Are we going to live in one of them?"

"Yes. No."

"Are there fireflies in New York, like home?" I liked to chase them around the big tree in our back yard. Susan could catch them but I never could.

"Maybe in the parks, but not on the streets," Mom answered.

"Will there be a big tree behind our house I can climb?"

"No. But you can go to the park and climb one."

"Are you sure about that, Mom?" Susan questioned.

"No."

I missed our tree. And our house and Grandpa, and Harry my friend, and Mingtoy, our dog. I squeezed down in my seat pretending I didn't care about New York anymore. But I secretly put my eyes just above the window ledge and gaped at the buildings. Suddenly, I realized I didn't know and blurted: "How do you get up in all the buildings? Walk?"

An army guy stood up from the seat in front of us just as my sister sneered, "Eeeh gods! You take an elevator."

"What's an elevator?"

"Hi, little guy! What's your name, soldier?"

"Tommy."

He stood up and came toward me. "Why don't you come up here and sit on my lap and I'll tell you what an elevator is."

I looked at Mom. She nodded.

"Hubba-Hubba!" Susan yelled.

He eyed her all the way down her body and shook his head. She got red in the face and threw herself into the seat on the other side of Mom and stared out the window.

He reached down and picked me up and swung around to his seat, put his arm around me and turned toward New York. He smelled just like Daddy.

"Where're you from?"

"Hutchinson, Kansas," Mom piped in. She was standing next to the seat, sort of guarding me I thought. I didn't need a guard! I was six!

"That near Topeka?" he wanted to know. "I got a buddy from Topeka."

"About fifty miles northwest of Wichita. Topeka is up near Kansas City."

"Gotcha!"

3

"Where's your home, Lieutenant?" She acted funny, like his mother.

"I see you know how to read rank. Where'd you learn that?"

"I just learned." I heard that little click in her voice she got when she talked about Daddy.

"Virginia, ma'am. I'm from Arlington, Virginia. It's a little town across the river from Washington, DC."

"Where the Department of Defense just opened."

His eyes got real big. My mom had a way of making men do that. Susan said it was because she was real smart and that men don't like smart women. Dumb.

He said his name was Franklin. Mom and Susan told him their names. Mom shook his hand and he got that funny look again.

He turned to me. "So, you've never seen an elevator, huh?" I shook my head.

"Well, an elevator is a box large enough for about ten people to stand up in. It has a very big wheel on the outside top part of the box with a fat steel rope around it. That wire rope goes all the way up to the top of the building and wraps around another big wheel screwed in the walls up there. When the elevator man pushes a handle, a motor pulls the rope and the box moves up. He can stop it at every floor and open the door and people can get out of the box or come in. When he pulls the handle, the box goes down. Get it?"

"No. What's that?" I pointed way out to a train without an engine. It was moving. This was getting really scary. Nothing looked right.

He laughed and hugged me. My face got hot. "That's a subway. It's a train but it runs on electricity instead of coal like this one. Don't worry, you'll learn all about the strange things in New York soon enough. Where's your dad? He in the service?"

Mom and Susan and I said, "He's" at the same time, but I finished first.

"He's killed." I never could get why everyone cried when they said that. I cried about Daddy sometimes at night in my bed. Still, I felt sorta good, no, proud, that he'd been killed fighting the Japs. But I wanted to find him in the sky and thought about that a lot; how to do that. The last time I'd seen him I didn't know it was the last time I'd see him.

"That's tough."

My mother moved into the seat next to us. She put her hand on my arm and told him, "My husband piloted one of the two B-26s that went down at Midway." Her hand trembled on me and she had that sound she always got when she said Daddy was killed—like she was gonna cry.

The train slowed down as New York got closer. My shirt was wet in the back it was so hot on the train. Franklin whispered things about New York in my ear and held me close. Susan pulled Mom back next to her. We all looked out the windows. Suddenly, we were out of the sun and the buildings were gone. I grasped Franklin's hand and looked around to find Mom. The lights came on in the train. A new smell pumped in the window with the coal soot. A wet smell. Susan squeaked and I thought I might cry. Mom and Franklin laughed.

"We're in a tunnel, Tommy," Franklin said. "We're going under the water between New Jersey and New York. The next time you see sun light you'll be on the street in Manhattan. You're a real New Yorker now."

CHAPTER 2

There are times when I don't know where I am. I've never told my mom about it, because she just talks and talks and tries to fix me when I only want her to listen to me. Like Daddy used to.

Once when I was five and walking home from kindergarten in Hutchinson, I could almost see my house, that's how flat everything was. I had to poop so I cut across a field to get home faster. I didn't make it and the poop came out in my pants. I cried and cried my shame for what I'd done, and couldn't understand why I hadn't been able to walk the straight line to my house.

In New York I got lost the first day of school. Susan walked me from our building to school—but I had to walk home myself. She said to go left out of school and left again at the corner and just walk two more blocks to our building. I knew my left and right but I turned right by mistake and then right again and couldn't see anything I knew. I was scared and wanted my daddy. I looked up in the sky for him and started to cry when I couldn't see him.

"Crying won't get you where you want to go," Mom always said. "It will just make a lot of mud and you'll get stuck." I sniffed hard and wiped my jacket across my eyes. She also said, "When you don't know, ask." My sister had shown me candy stores right after we got to New York. There was one right in front of me and I wondered if you could go in if you didn't have any money. I didn't but I went in.

Sweet smells more than a flower store enclosed me like Mom's afghan blanket when I'm cold. A fat lady in a dress with flowers stood behind the glass candy cases. Like every candy store, next to the cases was a soda fountain. I loved to sit on the circle stool seats and spin round and round. She stared down at me.

"Ah... I don't have any money." I was sure she'd kick me out.

"Nu? You think I'm gonna give you some?"

I felt like crying again but bit my lip real hard.

"I'm lost."

"Oy vey!" She changed from a money-candy-lady to a mother-lady. She came out from behind and knelt in front of me, smoothing my hair off my forehead. It always hung down over my eyes and Susan said I looked like a black-haired Yorkie. I didn't get it.

"What's your name, boychick?"

"Tommy."

"Okay, Tommy, you don't know your address by any chance."

"176 West 87th Street." I was proud I knew my address.

"A real smarty pants! It's not possible you know your phone number is it?"

"Trafalgar 4 4843." I smiled at her and she hugged me.

"Your building is right down this block, all the way at the end. You can maybe read numbers?"

"Sure! I'm six!"

"You want I should call your mother to come get you? What's with you out alone, anyway?"

"I'm walking home from school. My mom's at work."

"And you became lost, why? You talk peculiar. You're not from New York."

"Kansas. It's my first day. I made a mistake."

"So, you flew to school this morning?"

"My big sister took me but she told me to go home by myself: 'Left and left again at the corner.'"

She went back behind the cases, opened one, took out two pieces of candy and gave them to me.

***

This year, when I finished the second grade, something big happened to me: I met Fireman Mike. Don't ask me how, it just sorta happened.

First of all, now I'm allowed to go almost anyplace by myself after Mom makes sure I know the directions. I still get lost but I ask and people set me right. I travel all the way up to the Bronx to visit my grandpa and grandma and aunt and uncle—Daddy's family. I have to take three subways, a trolley and then walk a very long way to get to their house. The trolley is the funnest. I can go to the back of the car and turn the wheel and play motorman. Same thing coming home. It takes almost two hours each way so I always sleep over.

I love the loud subway and go to the front car and stand by the glass door and watch the track zoom up at us. I get penny gum from the gum and candy boxes on the poles in the stations. You put a penny in the little slit and there's a shiny metal handle at the bottom. You move it up into a slot that goes all the way across. You pick the candy or gum you want and push the handle down into that notch. Then you pull and the gum or candy drops into the tray. I always pick the Chiclet gum because there's two pieces in each box and I like the mint taste. None of my friends are allowed to go alone and one kid's mom said bad things about my mom when my friend made me tell her about my trips. I don't go there anymore.

It was summer and most of my friends were at camp or on vacation with their parents. I spent nearly every day alone, even made my own lunch when Susan wasn't home.

Often, I went up to the roof of our twelve-story building and looked out over New York. The roof was all covered with stinky black tar paper and I had to be careful where I stepped or I'd get gunk on my sneakers.

Up there I felt a lump in my throat most times and my shoulders and chest ached. I looked for my daddy out in the sky, but all I could see was New York stuff—the Hudson River, the George Washington Bridge, the big skyscrapers down town, and buildings taller than ours around our neighborhood. I could hear trucks and buses below and if I boosted myself up to the top of the wall that was all around the roof, I could lean over and see everyone walking on the streets, taking stuff from trucks to stores, getting on and off buses, even maids pushing little kids in strollers. Once or twice I saw people through the windows of other buildings. The sky above all that was empty of my daddy. Still, I could not stop feeling that, if I went higher, I would find him.

A water tower sat on the roof of our building; on all the buildings, actually. It was round with brown shingles and metal straps all the way around, and had a top like the roof of an African hut I'd seen in my geography book. A ladder began at the bottom, was screwed to the side and bent onto the roof to the very top of the tower. I wanted to climb that ladder and look through the window in the sky and finally see Daddy. But I was afraid to climb that high. It was much, much taller than the tree in Hutchinson and it looked dangerous. I tried to get up my courage. Someday soon, I promised.

Other days I walked up and down Broadway and watched the tough kids sneaking a ride by holding on to the bars on the back of trolleys. Sometimes the conductor would stop and race back to catch them, but they always got away; laughing as they sprayed in all directions away from the very mad conductor. I listened to the trucks and cars thumping over the cobblestones on Amsterdam Avenue, and played with the dogs that people walked along West End Avenue. Riverside Drive was boring except for the swings in the little park and the ships going along the Hudson. Central Park seemed too far away to me, although the trees and grass reminded me a little of Hutchinson. It made me sad to be in the park. The real problem, though, was that I had to cross Columbus Avenue to get to the park. It was well known that you not only did not walk along Columbus but tried not to cross it. There were so many tough kids there you were taking your life in your hands going on Columbus.

I stared in the windows of the butcher shop, the barber shop where I got my hair cut, the drug store, the hardware store, the florist, even the bank. Once in a while I visited Mom at the bookstore on 72nd Street where she worked. The people there all liked me but after a few minutes Mom had to "get back to work." Below 86th Street most of the buildings on Amsterdam were five-story brownstones. It was warm so women sat on the stoops and little kids played around them. I liked it when I saw kids and their parents together.

One day I was walking down Amsterdam and when I got to the corner of 83rd something very shiny red and gold flickered in the sunlight up the block. I looked hard and saw a red door with gold on it. A very strong force, like *The Shadow* (the guy on the radio show who can get invisible), pulled me up 83rd Street toward that door. As I got closer, I was amazed at what I saw: between two brownstones was a four-story narrow brick building with a very bright red door over the whole first floor. Actually, it was a garage door in the middle with a regular door on one side; all the wood was bright red. The cross logs were gold wood that was wavy instead of flat. At the very top was another strip of gold wood that looked like those ropes generals have over their shoulders in the Newsreels. Way up at the top above the garage door was a black sign with gold letters: *Engine Co. 74.*

What was this? What's "Co."? It looked more like Ali Baba's cave than a house. "Close your mouth, Tommy," I could hear my mother saying. I sure had my mouth hanging open in amazement. The buildings on both sides had open windows and a couple of women hung over the ledges waving magazines in front of their faces. Hot day. I smelled stew cooking close by and realized I'd forgotten to eat lunch.

Something touched me on the right shoulder. I looked and there was nothing there. Then another touch on my left shoulder. Again, nothing there. I turned around real quick and just caught sight of a smiling man jumping behind me trying to stop me from seeing him. What? This was a kid's game.

"What're ya doin,' kid? Are you a German spy?" The man looked like a giant.

"What? No! My dad was killed in the war. I'm no spy. Why're you touching me?"

"Just horsin' around. I didn't mean nothin' bad. You like the red door here?"

"Sure! But what is this building?"

"It's a firehouse."

"Whadayamean?"

He laughed and roughed up my hair. I looked into his bigness. His face was red, like he had a sunburn, but his arms were white with tons of freckles. His red hair was wavy. His muscles stuck out

13

of his black T-shirt so big he was almost scary. But he wasn't and I liked him right away.

"It's a building where we keep a fire engine. Like a garage but different."

"How?"

"It's got lots of fire equipment: buckets, and picks and extra hose and all our boots and suits and helmets. Stuff like that."

"'We?' You're a fireman?" All of a sudden I felt like I might float away.

"Yep. Name's Mike." He stuck out his huge hand. I shook, just like Daddy had shown me. Mike smiled a really big grin. I felt so little next to him.

"I'm Tom O'Neill. Tommy. Geez! A fireman! Why are you a fireman? Do you like fire? I like fire," I confided. "I always chased fireflies back in Kansas where I used to live. And once my friend, Ronnie and I took some matches and set fire to a field. Boy, did we ever get in trouble for that one." I giggled.

"That's not funny, Tommy." Mike's voice was low and stern, like he was gonna give me heck. I looked up at his face. He bent down on one knee on the sidewalk there. I could see the firehouse door and the sign, *Engine Co. 74* over his shoulder. "Fire is very dangerous stuff. It has its good uses, but it can kill ya. Twenty-eight firemen died in fires right here in New York just last year." His words were wiggly and sweat came on his forehead. His eyes looked sort of like he wanted to cry.

"What? What's wrong, Mike?"

"Aw, it's nothing.' Just something bad from the war."

"Were you in the war too? Like my daddy? He was a pilot at Midway. B-26. Shot down. Killed."

"You proud a that?" I got scared that he was mad and thought I was a bad boy."

"Well, er, ah, sort of. My daddy was doing something really big and good. Fighting the Japs. And Mom says that Midway was the start of when we won the war. Or something." I hung my head. I started to cry. I didn't know what to think.

Mike put a hand on my face and thumbed away a tear. "Don't cry, Tommy. You're right to be proud a your dad. He was doing a good thing and he died in a good cause. Don't be ashamed a that."

"Okay." I sniffed.

He stood up and took my hand. "You wanna see inside the fire house?"

"Yeah! You bet!"

CHAPTER 3

Mike said he should call my mom and ask her if it was okay to show me inside the firehouse. No adult ever did that with me before. I told him Mom's phone number at work. I hoped she wouldn't be mad, but I really wanted to see the fire engine. He opened the little door and used a phone on the wall. I tried to spy behind him, to see what was there but he blocked my view when he brought the telephone outside and closed the door.

"Hello, Mrs. O'Neill. My name is Mike Murphy. I'm a fireman at Engine Company 74 on 83rd Street, just down Amsterdam from you."

She must of said something, because he held his hand up like she was right there in front of him. "No, no. Tommy is right here and he's fine. He was hanging around outside looking at our bright red door like lots of boys do and I got to talking to him and asked if he wanted to take a look around inside. I thought I should ask your permission first. That's why I'm callin.'

"Okay. Yeah. No, the whole shift is here all the time. Never just one guy. Oh, yeah. I getcha. Good idea. I agree. Yeah." He listened. Then, "You

16

could come on down and go around with us if you want. After work, you know? Or you come first and decide if you want him to get a tour. No, no, we don't usually do this. It's just, well, I set myself when I got out of the Air Force….Yeah, Tommy said. Yeah, that too. I'm real sorry. I truly am, Mrs. O'Neill. I was in the Air Force in the Pacific too."

He listened.

"That is no difficulty. Well, like I was startin' to say, my life's goal is to teach kids to respect fire and avoid getting hurt by it."

He smiled and she talked.

"Really? That's swell! Sure. He won't be long. Do you want me to walk him home after?"

He frowned, like he just got it that I was allowed to go around by myself.

"Okay. If you say so. Send him back to us. He seems like a real nice kid. We like kids around here." He hung up.

"I can go?"

"Yep. Ready?"

I shook with anticipation. I felt like I was going into a fire-rescue world. All fire. Everywhere. Even on an airplane that had been hit by Jap fighter bullets or flak.

I'd seen lots of fire engines on the streets, but never up close, standing still so I could look at everything as close as I wanted. Mike stepped aside and opened the little door to let me in. It was much cooler inside. He reached to the wall and a million lights came on, like in one of the Broadway plays Mom took Susan and me to. I saw red and I heard

17

voices. Firemen's voices. Laughing and making jokes. I sniffed the air. Smoke! And damp, like the brownstone basement my friend had taken me to once.

The fire truck was different than I'd ever seen. Back in Kansas they still had a lot of fire wagons pulled by horses, and most trucks I'd seen in New York were old looking, like the Model T cars. Mom said that was because all new fire engines had been made for the war. Not this one. I guess my mouth was open again.

"A beauty, ain't she? Brand spankin' new Ward LaFrance Pumper. Carries five men. Pumps one thousand gallons per minute. Ladders on both sides, forty-feet of 'em in all. Ain't she just wonderful? Boy-oh-boy!"

"Yeah!" I looked at the red giant. It was like a god's chariot. "Gosh. What's that?" I pointed to a large, round gray metal bowl with a sorta wire with holes cover attached to the left front bumper.

"That, my son, is right from the war. It's a Q2B Siren. Biggest sound you're ever gonna hear on an emergency vehicle in this or any city. I'd turn it on but it'd blow your ear drums out."

"Really?"

"Yeah."

"Geez!"

"Look at them white-wall tires. Got a hose reel in the back. This is the best, Tommy."

I didn't know what to say. I was what my sister called, "speechless." I just stared. Finally, I asked, "Can I touch the fire engine?"

"Sure. Just don't pull or turn any knobs or anything like that. Get that thing started and you and I will have to jump in and drive it. It's got a mind of its own, like a big young horse." He laughed, throwing his head back and opening his mouth to the ceiling. I laughed too. Mike was funny. This was so fun.

I ran my hand over the front fender. It was smooth and shiny. I guess I looked a little surprised. I expected it would be rough and dirty from fires.

"We wash it down every mornin' regardless if we've had it out. All the houses do. Everywhere, I suppose."

I looked around. "Everything's so clean. Even the floor." He smiled.

I grasped a ladder rung and saw myself climbing right up the side of a skyscraper, all the way to the top. I wasn't afraid of heights. Except that water tower ladder, a little. Back in Hutchinson, I used to climb to the very top little branches of the big tree in our back yard which was taller than our house. No one in the neighborhood did that. The little kids were afraid and the big ones were too heavy to stand on the branches. It killed Susan that I could do something she couldn't.

"How high up do these ladders go?"

"With both sets we can get up to about the fourth floor."

"Four floors? Not all the way up?"

He laughed, like I was stupid for asking that. My face got hot. "The ladders are for rescuing people and getting to windows we have to knock out. We

19

hook the hose up to the fire plug and to the fire truck—the pumper. We pull the hose off the reel and carry it up the stairs to fight the fire. The pumper pushes the water through the hose. And, the Department has ladder trucks that come and raise their ladders way up, about seven stories up.

"But...what about the really tall buildings? What if there's a fire, say, on the twentieth, or fiftieth floor? Don't they have really tall ladders for those?" I felt like crying and didn't know why. It was a dumb question; something I should know. How come I didn't know?

"Most people ask that question, Tommy. How tall is your building?"

"Twelve stories." Even a fire on our floor— the ninth—the firemen couldn't get ladders to us. We'd burn. Daddy's plane came into my eyes "going down in flames" as Susan had said. Was he shot dead in his pilot's seat by a Jap fighter plane, or was his plane gunned down into the ocean by flak from a Jap ship? Did his plane blow up and he got burned up?

"We'd bring the hose up the stairs to you. And our Ward LaFrance pumper here can shoot water outside higher than your building to a fire on high floors. Anyway, almost all apartment fires in the tall buildings are in one room. Wallpaper and furniture. Very few spread to whole floors of buildings, especially the older buildings like yours."

"Why?"

"Because those are made of concrete walls and that stops the fires from spreading around."

20

I looked up at his strong face; his dark red hair appeared brown next to the bright fire truck. I didn't understand what he was saying.

"But the hoses are heavy and what if the elevator is burned? How would you get up to my floor? My teacher says there's more than seven million people in New York, so I figure thousands and thousands are burned up every year...." I was crying really hard and fell against Mike's chest as he dropped to his knees in front of me.

"Shhhh. Shhhh." He put his arms around me and stroked the back of my head. "What's this all about? You ever been in a fire?"

"No." I sniffed and tried to stop crying.

"You ever seen anyone get hurt in a fire?"

"In the movies."

"Oh. That's just pretend. Those people don't really get hurt."

"I seen it in the Newsreel."

"What'd you see?"

"I saw whole buildings burning in Germany and Japan." Mike took his arms away and fell back against the big tire of the fire engine. I said, "And I saw a lot of big army airplanes flying and black smoke puffs around them. My mother said it was flak from anti-aircraft guns. Then one plane got hit and I saw fire and I saw the whole plane go down." I cried and just put my own arms around myself and rocked.

"What?" He was back at me.

"My daddy was in a plane and got shot like that. Burned by the fire." I couldn't stop crying and just wanted to go up in the sky and find him, maybe even be with him.

Again Mike put his huge arms around me and I cried on his shirt. "I know, Tommy. I know."

"How do you know? Did your daddy get killed too? Like that?"

"No. But...." His voice choked. I pulled my face back and looked into his. It was all twisted up and red. He looked at my eyes with a question in his. "I know about death by fire, Tommy."

I waited for him to go on but he just opened his mouth like he was going to speak and then closed it and shook his head and then opened and closed it again. "I can't," he said. "I have a big secret but I can't tell you." He shook some and I realized he was crying. I'd never seen a man cry, except Daddy when he left that last time and that was only tears in his eyes. This was big crying. I wanted to make him stop so I tried to hug him but his shoulders were so big I couldn't get very far around them. I heard the men upstairs joking and I got afraid they'd come down and see Mike this way.

"Don't cry, Mike. You can tell me your secret. Or not. I'll keep it secret. I promise. Cross my heart and hope to die." I Xed over my heart. I put my hands on his cheeks and got him to look at me. He seemed more like a kid than ever. Something was wrong with him and this was it.

"Mike?"

He looked at me for a moment, then his eyes rolled way back. "I can't get them all out of my eyes.

22

Especially at night. And when planes go over, I want to run and hide."

"I hate planes too. You know why."

"Yeah. I know, Tommy." He sighed and pulled himself back up and ruffled my hair. "I'm okay, buddy. Thanks for the hug. It's nice to have someone understand somewhat. Even a little guy like you." He laughed and so did I. "Maybe one day I'll be able to tell you. I'd like you to be the one. I feel like you would keep my secret and I surely need to tell someone. Definitely."

CHAPTER 4

After that, I went to the firehouse almost every day. I didn't tell Mom all the time, 'cause I thought she might get mad since Mike is a man and I'm a kid. But Mike was different than any man I'd ever met. He was sorta like a kid. A big man and a fireman, sure, but the look on his face was odd. A lot of times he didn't seem like he knew what to say or do. You know, adults just do what they want, move around where and when they like. Not like kids. We stand there (even on the street) and can't decide what to do next, or where to go next. And when we talk with other kids, we often together don't know what we want to do. Mike was like us. I don't know how to explain it. He was sorta like a man-kid. Like a big brother but not as mature as he was old. Especially seeing he'd been in the war.

I liked him a lot. He showed me all around the firehouse, introduced me to the other firemen, let me slide down the fire pole and even sit in the driver's seat of the truck. He told me millions of things about firefighting. I was definitely going to be a fireman when I grew up. He said he'd show me the way. Then he squinted out into the distance, pulled his lower lip under his upper teeth and said, "But only if the reason you're doing it is 'cause you want to save kids and teach kids about fire and being careful." I nodded even though I didn't really feel that way. Anyone killed in a fire was the same to me, except fliers in wars. I didn't feel anything except excitement from the pictures in my head of climbing ladders, smashing windows, carrying people out over my shoulder, blasting a room full of fire with hosed water, and driving the truck. Well, everything!

One day Mike found out I didn't know how to play baseball or even catch a ball; he practically jumped up and down. "What? You kidding me? Oh, right, you got no dad or brothers. Your uncle in the Bronx never taught you? Your grandpa? No? Well, we gotta fix that." He told me to ask my mom for a baseball glove.

***

"What about your father's?" She dug it out of somewhere and showed me. I took it to Mike. "That's great, Tommy, but it's real old fashioned. Now they got new mitts. Ask her. Say, 'fielder's glove,' and ask if I can come and advise when you go to the store."

So a few days later, the three of us marched down Broadway to Davega's sport store. I walked out with a Rawlings fielder's glove—two fingers and a thumb. It fit great, Mike said. I also got a brand new baseball. Boy! I wanted to laugh and yell and run all the way home and back to them I was so excited. The kids all played ball, but since I didn't even know how to catch, I never got asked. "Don't they have balls in Kansas?" they teased me. Everyone laughed and I got red in the face. I wanted Daddy more then than most other times.

Behind the firehouse there was a kind of big alley and Mike took me there. He put the glove on my hand. "Like this: when the ball's comin,' stick the glove out to meet it. When you feel it hit the pocket, squeeze the glove closed so it doesn't drop out. In front of you for balls coming at your stomach and above. Balls below the waist tip the glove down and open. Open and out to the left for balls that way and backhand balls to the right side of your body."

I wanted to throw up. I didn't think I'd ever get it. But I was determined and Mike showed me over and over, day after day, first tossing the ball underhanded and eventually throwing it overhand with a soft arc, and finally actually having a real catch with me. My arm was sore at first but then toughened up. I couldn't wait for my friends to come home from vacation.

At noon on a hot August day, sitting against the back wall of the firehouse, eating ham-on-rye with mustard and coleslaw sandwiches and drinking Pepsi, Mike said, "You sure your mom's okay with all the times you come here?"

"Sure. Why not?"

"You answered that just a little too quick mister man. You're lying. What? You haven't told her? What does she think you're doing with your glove and ball every time you take 'em out of the apartment?"

I didn't say anything for a while, trying to think of a story he'd believe.

"What're you afraid of? She'd yell at you? Hit you?"

"No! Are you kidding? My mom? Hit? Scream? My friends' moms, yeah, but not mine. She never yells or hits. Not once can I remember. At my sister either."

"Boy! How's she get you to do what you're supposed to do? What about when you're bad or fight with Susan or spill something or just for nothing? Like my mom and dad. And big sister. Jeez! They yellin' all the time. I got whacked plenty when I was a kid."

I didn't actually have an answer. That's just not how my mom was. "She doesn't have to yell," I finally said. "If I do something wrong she just calls my name if I'm in the other room. 'Thomas?' I know 'Thomas' means cut it out. Or if I get a note home from school for fooling around, I have to sit on the sofa while she reads it. Funny, she's a fast reader but she sure reads those notes slow. Makes me sweat. Then she'll say something like, 'I'm surprised at you, Tom.' If I'm really bad, which is almost never, she'll say, 'Tommy, your father would be ashamed of you.' All those words get to me. Anyway, I want to be good for her. I hear her crying for Daddy sometimes at night when she thinks I'm asleep. I can't sleep so good." Whew! I'd told Mike a lot of stuff I'd never told anyone. It scared me.

"So what about your dad?"

"Whadaya mean?" My heart banged.

"You never said one word about him after that first day. Why not?"

"I don't know. I don't like to think about him too much."

"Why? I thought you were proud of him. Getting killed fighting the Japs and all that."

"I am." I didn't want to cry again. I thought about what I could say, about what I wanted to say, what I was willing to say. Not a lot. I looked around the alley. Garbage cans behind each building. The brownstones all had fire escapes in the back there. Some had flower pots just outside the window. A couple even had clothes lines between them and the back of the buildings on 82nd Street. How did they work that? "It's just...I don't know." I rubbed my chest with my chin and picked at the dirt under my fingernails, wondering where it all came from. "I just don't understand where he went. You know?"

"Yeah! I do know."

"I mean, okay, if flak hit his plane and it blew up and he was burned up, where did he go? Where is he? Just a bunch of pieces down at the bottom of the ocean? Eaten by sharks?" I was trembling bad now. "I remember when he hugged me last. A long, long time ago. I was only four but I remember. I looked at his face and he had his eyes closed and I could feel his heart against mine. But I could feel something else. Something besides his body. I never forgot it. And I keep thinking that that part of him sorta blew out of him when his body died; that it went into the sky and is floating around and if I go high enough I'll be able to see him. I used to climb up our tree in Hutchinson and look for him. So now I wanna go to the Empire State Building and I think I'll see him. It's like I'm

supposed to see him and I'm bad because I haven't."
I stopped shaking and finally looked up at Mike.
"Dumb, huh?"

Mike had tears in his eyes. He reached out a
big hand and put it on my head. "Not dumb, Tommy.
Not dumb at all. Pretty damned smart if ya ask me."

We sat for a while, going back to our
sandwiches and Pepsis. Mike kept staring at the back
of the firehouse like he was trying to figure something
out.

"You know, Tommy. I think I know how you
can get the answers to all your questions."

CHAPTER 5

I felt pretty confused after leaving Mike that day. He'd taken me to a man and made me tell him everything about Daddy and the other stuff. Mike didn't even stay while I talked to the man. I didn't mind. The man was kind and listened to me and told me some secrets about death and urged me to keep looking for my father up in the sky. And some other things too. He made me feel a little better but I wasn't sure I believed what he told me.

***

That night we had corn on the cob for dinner. Nothing else. I loved those dinners. We used to do that in Kansas all the time. Corn country, everyone said. This corn was different, though. It had little kernels that popped out with just a tiny pressure from your teeth, and tasted sweet like milk. We had silver corn holders from our dead grandma and Mom let us put our whole cob on the block of butter and roll it around as much as we wanted. Butter-dripping corn. The best! We all loved it and just sat at the table rolling corn, salting it and munching away, ear after ear. Susan and I even spoke through the crunches though other times we weren't allowed to talk with food in our mouths.

30

I wanted to ask Mom about what the man said but Susan was jabbering away. I could hardly understand her through the bites. "Mom..." crunch, crunch. "Can I..." chomp, chomp, "get a pair..." slurp, burp, "of falsies?"

I didn't know what "falsies" were but Mom did. It was something important because she stopped gnawing her own corn, put it down on her plate, wiped her mouth, took a drink of water and said, "Absolutely not!"

"Why not? All the girls have biggies except me. It's humiliating. I haven't even gotten my...."

"That's enough! There is such a thing as the right not to hear and in this case Thomas has it."

Oops! "Thomas!" Uuuuuuu! Must be huge. "The right not to hear?" I almost ate my corn cob. Could I use that in school? "What're falsies?" I asked. I knew what "biggies" were. Susan loved to shock everyone by saying the words for body things. She also pranced around in her angora sweater with her chest out asking me and Mom if we could see her "biggies." "Not yet," Mom would say and Susan would throw herself into the closest chair.

"See what you've unleashed?" Mom said.

"What's the big deal if he knows? Besides, what's wrong with big biggies, however I get 'em, when all the boys like 'em so much?"

"I don't know why boys your age like them so much. Probably because they're infantile, as in still fixated on their mother's breasts."

"Mom!"

31

"Clear the table and do the dishes. I'm listening to the news." With that, she pushed her chair back and went into the living room for her nightly ritual of world news and one or two evening shows, like, *Ellery Queen, Boston Blackie*, and *Ginny Simms*. She liked mysteries and music.

I was nervous while clearing and drying the dishes—Susan never let me wash. She was singing some stupid love song she'd learned from the radio. *"Let that pair of golden earrings cast their spell tonight."* I was thinking. I was scared to tell Mom about the man but had to know what to think and knew she could help me. Funny, I never really talked about Daddy and all to her before. Not to anyone except Mike and the man. The few times I had mentioned Daddy to Susan she'd burst into song:

"...We live in fame...
Go down in flame,
Nothing'll stop the Army Air Corp."

Then she'd turn away and stare at something. I couldn't tell her anything!

A fire engine wailed down nine stories. I wondered if it was Mike's and if he was on it. A stab of fear knifed my chest.

Later, when Susan's friend Judy had come over and they'd gone to her room and Mom was reading, I went into the living room and sat on the davenport. We didn't have wallpaper so the walls would be okay in case of fire. But we had draperies from the ceiling to the floor and a huge carpet that covered the whole room. Those would burn fast. "Plan your escape now, before there's a fire," Mike had said. "So you can crawl in the right direction in case there's a lot of smoke." There was no fire escape on our building, so we'd have to make it out the front or back doors of our apartment and down the stairs. Mike said the elevators would be shut down if there was a fire. My room was next to the kitchen and the back door so I could get out that way. But Mom and Susan had bedrooms down the hall past the living room and dining room. I'd have to go get them and guide them to the front door. As long as it wasn't blocked by fire.

Mom looked up and I guess seeing I didn't have a book or anything asked, "What is it Tommy? Something's bothering you. I could see it all evening." I was always amazed when Mom did that—saw inside me.

"Well, ah, Grandma said I'm going to hell 'cause I wasn't baptized and didn't take First Communion and all." That surprised even me since I wanted to tell her something else.

"What? That old biddy. She's the one who's going to burn in hell for torturing a child." She was mad.

"She calls you a kike sometimes. She even once said to Aunt Margaret when they thought I was asleep that 'Hitler missed one with her.' They were talking about you. I wanted to yell at them but I didn't. I thought she'd hit me. Do I have to go there again?"

"Never. You hereby have my permission to wash your grandmother and aunt right out of your mind. Don't even go to their funerals, may they come quickly." I'd never seen her so mad. She actually got up and went in the kitchen and came back with a glass of ice. She got a bottle of some sort of whiskey out of the cabinet in the living room and poured some in her glass. Holy moly!

After a few swallows, she squinted at me. Here she goes looking into me again, I thought. "There's something else, isn't there? C'mere." She beckoned and I sat at her feet. She put her hand on my forehead and stroked backwards through my hair; one of my favorite things. "Don't be afraid, Tommy. You never have to be afraid of telling me anything."

I picked at the carpet and looked around the room at the old paintings on the wall. "Okay. Well, you know Mike, right?"

"Sure. Has something happened to him?"

"Nah. Well, I sorta told him about Daddy and stuff…."

"Whadayou mean, 'and stuff?'"

I'd never told her this and was scared to but I just had to. I bit my cheeks and crossed my fingers. "About how he got blown up dead and just disappeared into the sky and I've been thinking I can find him and see him up there." I was crying now. "If I go high enough."

She slid down onto the floor next to me, wrapped her arms around me, pulled me across her lap like a baby, and kissed me on the forehead between hugs. That made me cry more.

"Did Daddy ever cry? Would he be mad or ashamed of me if he saw me crying?"

34

"Sure he cried. He was a regular old crybaby. Sad movies, news of people dying, things we heard about what Hitler was doing to the Jews in Germany. You name it, he cried over it. But what's this got to do with Mike?" She sounded a little suspicious and I sat up, turned around and sat cross-legged and looked right at her. She was so beautiful to me. She said her face was long and her ears too big, but her large brown eyes were a place I jumped into when I needed...anything.

"He took me to a man who told me the answers to my questions about Daddy. And the man said Daddy is in heaven and that if I came to his building he could help me see Daddy."

"What? What kind of man? What sort of building?" She got up into her chair and took another big swallow of her drink. Her face colored pink and a little blue line I'd never seen before went up and down on her forehead.

"A priest. Father Joe. In the church on 71st Street near Broadway." I talked fast, hoping to avoid what I knew was coming.

"What? A priest? In a Catholic church? And he talked to you about heaven and your father? And Mike took you there?"

"Yes," I whispered.

She was back in her chair, tapping her fingernails on the table with the drink on it. Her lips were pulled tight together like she'd just eaten a lemon. I sat, frozen.

35

Finally, she got up and went to the phone, picked it up and dialed. I hoped, hoped that she wasn't calling Father Joe. He'd really been nice to me.

"Is Michael Murphy there, please?" Butter wouldn't melt in her mouth, but I knew better. She didn't yell but she could be tough. However, I'd never seen her like this. How did she know the number? She'd even memorized it. "I'll wait." She clicked her fingernails again, this time on the telephone table. She stood instead of sitting on the little stool that was there. I just knew this was the end of Mike and me. Please don't, Mom!

Mike must have come to the phone. "Mr. Murphy? This is Tommy's mother, Mrs. O'Neill." She sounded very polite and nice. "Okay, 'Mike' then. I'd like you to come to our apartment for dinner as soon as you can. You've been so nice to Tommy I thought it would be good to get to know one another a little better. And for you to meet Tom's sister, Susan." Susan! Uh-oh!

CHAPTER 6

Two days before Mike was coming over, Mom, Susan and I were planning. Well, they were planning and I was sticking my two cents in every once in a while. I was afraid they'd mess it up. Mike was a guy's-guy and never talked about having a girlfriend and wasn't that easy around the few women I'd seen him talk to.

"It's so hot," Susan complained. We were in the living room, the draperies open and the two windows up; the grey stone of the building next door looked like one of those modern paintings at that museum downtown that Mom took us to.

Mom answered, "We'll put one floor fan at each end of the dining room table. That should help a little. Anyway, we're all hot all the time, including Mike, I'm sure."

"What about the table fan?" I wanted to know. I felt like this was my party because Mike was my friend, you know?

"We'll put that in the living room for before dinner," Mom said. "Right next to the davenport where I'll put Mike. Now, what's for dinner?"

"He's Irish," Susan offered. "What do they eat? Corned beef and cabbage?" She giggled. I wanted to punch her on the arm.

"I could do a prime rib and roast potatoes and a Waldorf salad." Mom had an arm across her middle holding her other elbow. Her hand was on her chin.

"No!" I yelled. They both jumped.

"What?" Susan asked.

"He's not a fancy guy. He'd be, I don't know…." I couldn't find the right words.

"Embarrassed?" Mom suggested.

"Yeah. We should have regular food, like spaghetti and meatballs and bread and butter."

Mom and Susan looked at each other. Susan snickered. Mom held her palms up.

"Okay. If that's what you want."

Oh, good! She actually took my idea. Yay!

Then they started on how the dinner table should be set. They wanted good linen and thin glasses and "the sterling, of course." I panicked. I knew Mike wouldn't be able to even talk if they did that. How was Mom going to "get to know him" if he felt like he didn't belong here?

"Please, Mom," I begged. "Just the place mats and paper napkins and kitchen glasses and knives and forks and spoons. How about ice cream for dessert? I know he likes that. He's taken me." I knew I was talking very fast but I couldn't help it. If they did this wrong, Mike probably wouldn't want me around anymore.

Susan threw up her hands and left the room, but Mom came to me, put her arms around me, kissed me on the head and said, "I understand, Tommy. I guess you know Mike a lot better than we do. You're right and I'm proud of you for knowing those things and having the courage to tell us. It's going to be a fine evening. I'll watch you and you signal me if I'm doing anything wrong. I can't account for Susan, though." We both laughed and I hugged her back.

***

So that fateful Friday night came. I felt like I had two families and they were just meeting for the first time. Which was true, but another thing was that if my first family didn't like my second one, I'd probably lose number two. Like I've said before, Mike was a little like a man-child. It didn't bother me or even show that much when he and I were hanging out, but the very fact that he liked to be with me so much was a little strange. I was really, really worried about the dinner. I woulda prayed but I didn't know if I actually believed in God so that wouldn't work. I just kept my fingers crossed and tried to be extra nice to Mom and Susan.

"Ring, ring." Mike looked huge in the frame of the door when Mom opened it. Susan stood just behind, peering over her shoulder. Mike had on a shirt and tie and shined shoes and slicked-down hair. I'd never seen him like that. He was all nice and polite, but I could see his eyes darting around, even in the foyer, and knew he felt out of place. This was not how his family lived. I knew this was a mistake. I wanted to reassure him that we were regular people like his family, but then I remembered some of the things he'd said about his mom and knew we were not like them.

Susan was wide-eyed and all smiles. Mike was a good looking guy and she really noticed it. I half expected her to stick her chest out and ask him if he could see her biggies. She was flirting, though. As everyone introduced themselves and we moved into the living room, I saw Susan squeezing her eyelids together, just a speck, as if she was trying to get Mike into better focus, as if something about him didn't fit.

Mom offered him a beer or whiskey but he said he didn't drink alcohol. I had told her so! "Cokes for the three kids," she said. Susan took over while Mom was getting the drinks.

"So, Mike, do you have a girlfriend?" Good thing I wasn't drinking my soda, I would have spit it out.

"Nope. I had one before I joined the Air Force, but I was only seventeen then. 'Spose I should get one, huh, Susan?"

She blushed. "Of course you should. Seventeen. How old are you? You look seventeen now."

"Twenty. People always say I look young. My mom says if I wasn't so big they probably wouldn't let me in to see all the movies." He laughed. I laughed. Susan frowned.

She asked, "What high school did you go to?"

"Stop being so nosy," I snapped.

"No, Tommy. It's okay. After all I'm here so's your family can get to know me better, right? I went to George Washington near our apartment in Washington Heights."

Mom came in with the bottles of Coke, passed them out and sat in her chair. She had a glass of whiskey and ice. I wondered if she was nervous too. Susan was on the other chair and Mike and I were on the davenport.

"You were in the army, right?" Susan was trying to find out something but I didn't know what.

"Army Air Force."

"Did they draft you?"

"I enlisted and lied about my age. They needed guys so they didn't press too hard on the birth certificates, if you know what I mean."

"Ah! So you didn't graduate high school!"

"Susan!" Mom said. "Where are your manners? Go put the butter on the table and pour the ice water. My goodness. I thought I raised you better than that. Excuse her, Mike. Really!"

"It's okay, Mrs. O'Neill."

"Claire, please. No formalities here."

"Okay, er, ah, Claire. Gosh, I don't think I can get used to that. Calling an adult by her first name."

"Well, I can see you were taught your manners. Not like some people I know." She called that last part to Susan in the dining room.

"Well," Mike said, sort of laughing. "I learned my manners from the back of my mother's hand you might say."

No one said anything for a little while.

"I think it's time for dinner," Mom said and got up to lead the way. "Wash your hands, Tommy."

"I'll go with you," Mike said.

***

"That smells really good," Mike pronounced when Mom brought the big bowl of spaghetti and sauce and meatballs to the table.

"Do you like a big spoon with your spaghetti, Mike?" Mom asked. He didn't answer 'cause he didn't know what she was talking about.

I said, "You know, to twirl your spaghetti so it's a nice tight wad."

"Oh, yeah. I seen that. No, thank you. We just twirl in our plates and bite off the stragglers." He blushed and giggled and we all laughed.

"Great idea!" Susan squealed. "Can I do that, Mom?" We weren't allowed "stragglers." Mom said it was bad manners.

"Of course," Mom granted, as if "who would think differently?" Boy, Susan could sure see the tiniest crack in anything and slither through it if it gave her an edge up. I thought she was going to be a criminal when she grew up. I didn't know any other profession where she could use that.

Everyone was served up, the bread and butter and grated cheese were passed and we all chowed down. Mike took great heaping amounts on his fork, bent to get a mouthful and chomped down on the dangling strands so they dropped back into the plate. It looked like fun and soon Susan and I were imitating him, all of us looking up from our plates at the other two and giggling, then laughing a lot so we had to put down our forks and double over. I fell on the floor I was laughing so hard.

"I think I'm peeing my pants!" Susan screamed and Mike and I grunted, gurgled and squeezed out painful sounds we were laughing so hard.

"Susan!" Mom reprimanded.

"I can't help it, Mom!" she said through her gasps. She was grabbing herself between the legs. I began to worry she really was going to pee in her pants and that Mike would be disgusted, but it seemed funnier than threatening so I just laughed some more until I burped a big one and that set the uproar off again. Poor Mom. She just sat there smiling, nodding now and then toward each of us, not having any idea what we were laughing at. And neither did we. That was what was so funny.

Finally, we all calmed down and Mike and Mom began to talk. We were all finished except for Mike who was on his third helping. They talked about baseball a little. I guess Mom had read the paper or something since she didn't ever talk about it before. "Tommy's father was a huge Cardinal fan. Dizzy Dean? 'The Gas House Gang?' Do you know those?"

"Sure! 1934 world champs. Everyone's heard of them. I'm a Yankee fan, myself, especially being so close to Yankee Stadium and all growin' up. We could get into the games for a quarter. Depression, you know?"

"Yes. We know all about the Depression in Kansas." Mom got tears in her eyes, like she was remembering something hard from before I was born. I'd heard stories....

After baseball came firefighting and Mike's job. I was beginning to get a little bored and even Susan had cleared the table all on her own and was in the kitchen doing the dishes, singing at the top of her lungs so's Mike would be impressed. Girls! He didn't seem to notice and was paying attention to everything Mom said, like she was his school teacher. She told him about Kansas and our life there, about Daddy, and her job at the bookstore. She asked a lot about his family. He still lived at home. His dad and mom had worked in a clothes factory during the war making uniform shirts.

"Which brings me to something, Michael," she finally said. Oh, oh. Here it comes. He was still eating. "I understand that you took Tommy to see a priest recently."

"That's right. Tommy told me he was having trouble figuring out about what had happened to his dad when he got shot down, you know? So I figured the priest could set him straight. Seein' as you're Catholic and all. I hope that was okay." He forked a last glob of spaghetti into his mouth.

"Actually, we're Jewish," Mom said.

Mike stopped chewing and a long strand of spaghetti dangled from his lips as his eyes opened wide and looked like blue quarters. His face was down near his plate. But he couldn't seem to bite the spaghetti strand. I began to think he might be having some sort of heart attack or something. He just stared at Mom and she stared back at him, like she half expected he might say something bad about Jews.

At just that moment, Susan came in with a big bowl of ice cream and four little bowls. She stopped at the doorway, looked around and said, "What happened?"

Mike bit and slurped. Mom took a sip of her ice water and I was so nervous that the spaghetti sauce burned in my stomach. I felt like throwing up.

"Jewish!" Mike managed. "But, O'Neill?"

"My husband was Catholic, but a non-believer. His mother drove him from his faith. He used to say, 'If the church can't see the evil in that woman and still lets her in, I'm out.' No, Michael, the Catholic Church has already created enough grief for me—trying to stop my marriage, going after my children—not that my own family was exactly overjoyed and embracing when it came to my marrying Tommy's father...." Her voice trailed away as if in a bad dream. I'd seen her do this before, but this was about something I'd never heard.

"I'm sorry, Mrs. O'Neill. I didn't know. I'll never do anything like that again. I promise." He sounded like Susan and I and we both looked at him to see why he was talking like that. A kid in a man's body, like I said.

***

Later, after Mike had gone, Mom came in and sat on the edge of my bed. It was so hot that the sheets felt wet. She had brought in the table fan for me.

"I like Mike," she said.

45

"Me too."

"I can see why. He's like a pal more than a grown man."

"I know. Why is that?"

"My guess is that something happened to him in the war. He saw something, maybe, something that drove him back to childhood, away from the terrible world of adults where men butcher one another."

"Oh."

"No more priests, you hear?"

"Yeah. But what about my question? Where's Daddy?"

"I don't know, Tommy. He's dead. That's all."

"So, is he in heaven or not?"

"Not."

CHAPTER 7

It's not like all I did was think about Daddy and death and Mike. There were a few kids who hadn't gone away, mainly Puerto Rican guys, and I got friendly with the ones who lived on my block. One especially—Henry Ruiz—became my really best friend. He was a great ballplayer and taught me a lot about taking grounders on one hop and making side-armed throws across the diamond. He played third base whenever there was a game. The Puerto Ricans didn't seem to like to go the three long blocks from Amsterdam to Central Park so they mainly played stick ball in the street. I couldn't hit anything, even the ones they started to lob softly to me. They called me "The Strike Out King." I knew they liked me anyway.

We played stoop ball, box ball, wall ball, ring-a-levio, had tons of baseball catches, ate candy and drank egg creams. They didn't seem to care that I was Jewish or I that they were Puerto Ricans. Most of my friends' mothers didn't want them playing with "spics," and since I did, a few thought maybe their boys shouldn't play with me. It all seemed dumb.

I still went to the firehouse and played catch and talked with Mike, and whenever I heard a plane, I looked up, and never gave up thinking I should go high and try to see Daddy. I knew I wasn't the only kid who had lost his father but that didn't matter. It was like he was a ghost walking around looking for a resting place; a place only I could give him when I figured out what really happened to him after his body died. I sometimes talked to Mike about it, but even though he was a Catholic and they believed in heaven and hell and all that, he wasn't sure. He told me so. It had something to do with his secret, which he still wouldn't tell me. I pushed a little every once in a while but he just changed the subject.

It was getting close to the end of the summer and some of my friends came back from camp and vacation. They were amazed and glad that I had learned to play baseball. Well, at least to catch and throw. I still didn't know how to bat and wasn't sure about most of the rules, but they were always arguing with each other about the rule for something that happened in our games so I didn't have to know much.

"Mike wants to take you up to his parents' home for dinner Sunday noon," Mom said one night when I came in all sweaty from playing ring-a-levio with Henry and my other Puerto Rican friends.

"Did he call?"

"Yes. Just a little while ago. So?"

"Sure! Yeah! I want to go. I gotta see this family he lives in."

"What do you mean?"

"Well, he said his mom and sister and even his dad are yellin' and screamin' all the time and he used to get hit if he didn't do what he was supposed to. But they all still love each other. Sounds like the circus." I was laughing and very excited about going; about being invited by an adult to his family's house for dinner.

Mom tried to make me dress up on Sunday but I knew that would be wrong for Mike's family. I wanted to wear dungarees and a baseball shirt. We finally compromised with school pants and a collar shirt and school shoes instead of sneakers. Combed hair, scrubbed fingernails. She also insisted that I take a bunch of carnations to his mother. She got 'em. I carried 'em.

"Now remember, Mike is Catholic like your Grandma O'Neill, although he doesn't seem dogmatic like her. But you're Jewish and don't let anyone push you around or try what the priest did. Mike will help you, I'm sure."

Suddenly, I was nervous about something I hadn't even thought about before. Nah! I wasn't gonna let that spoil my good time. I couldn't wait to see what we had for dinner.

Sunday came and Mike picked me up. He smiled when he saw how I was dressed and I thought he was laughing at me. Mom pushed me out the door and we were on our way.

"Boy, my Mom's sure gonna be impressed with you, buddy boy. Oh, and flowers! She'll probably throw me out the window and take you in as her new son. Extra desert for you, mister." I laughed. I guessed I could take getting teased a little.

When we walked out the door of my apartment building, life changed. Mike took my hand. I started to pull away. What did he think: I needed to hold hands when we were crossing the street? Not me! His big, calloused hand oozed sweat onto mine, even though it wasn't that hot. What was this? Mike, the fireman was scared? What?

He babbled as we walked to the train; about everything and nothing. The August late morning heat was beginning to rise off the sidewalks. We got on the 7th Avenue Local at 86th and Broadway. Descending the stairs, hot air, heated since May, rushed up at us, carrying the usual stinks of pee, sweaty bodies, dry newspapers, engine oil and electricity. Mike talked on and clung to me. I was a little embarrassed but began to understand more deeply that Mike was afraid to go to his apartment, afraid of his parents and sister; of something there that I might see. I thought he must be sorry he invited me. He held on to me like a buddy-guard; "strength in numbers." The more I thought that, the more scared I got. What was there? What could I do? How could I protect him?

We got out at 168th Street and Broadway and started walking toward the East River. He'd told me we'd have to walk a few blocks to his apartment.

"Here's somethin' for ya, pal," he said when we came out of the subway. "Right here, on this land, is where the New York Yankees had their first baseball park back in 1903. Called 'Hilltop Park.' They were called the Highlanders in those days. All the big names of the American League played here. Bet you never heard of Ty Cobb." I shook my head. "Cy Young?" No again. "I got a lot to teach you about baseball history, Tommy."

We walked four blocks over to Edgecombe Avenue and 167th Street. I could feel we were going downhill and figured that's why they called the baseball place 'Hilltop Park.'

The neighborhood was a lot dirtier and poorer than mine. There were no big apartment buildings either. Most apartment buildings I'd been in, including ours, hadn't been painted since before the war. That made everything look crummy. Mike's looked worse.

I was amazed that his building had a self-service elevator. I'd never seen one before. I asked Mike about it and he said they were in poorer buildings with more than four floors. "Cheaper for the landlord than paying for an elevator man." I guess I thought he lived in a brownstone walk-up. They lived on the fourth of five floors.

When Mike opened the door with his key we were right in the living room. Everyone was there.

"Mom and Pop," Mike said, this here is Tommy, the kid I been telling you about. Best kid in the neighborhood.

"C'mon in big guy," Mike's father boomed. "Mike says you're a Yankee fan."

"Well, er, sort of. Sure. I'm just learning about baseball. Mike's teaching me."

"Dodgers are the only team," a man said.

"Get outa here!" Mr. Murphy shouted.

"That's Charley, my sister's boyfriend," Mike interrupted. "And that's Shelia, my sister."

"Hiya!" Charley waived to me from the davenport. Squirty little guy in a brown shirt with no tie. Brown pants and shoes and his hair was slicked back with no part.

"Pleased to meetcha," Shelia remarked. Her lipstick was bright red and there was a lot of it. She wore a light blue angora sweater like my sister, Susan. But she had biggies. Plenty of them.

I shook hands with everyone, like Mom had said.

"Last and best, here's my mom."

"Hello, Mr. and Mrs. Murphy." I pulled the flowers from behind my back where I'd been hiding them and gave them to her.

"Thank you, Tommy! No one around here ever brings me flowers." She glared at her children and husband. "Get out! All a youse! It's just Tommy and me from now on." She grinned at me.

"Told you," Mike said, grinning too.

Mrs. Murphy pulled me into her big bosom for a hug. She smelled like cooking and a small moist patch of sweat wet my cheek. Her hair was gray and pulled back behind her head. She didn't have on any lipstick or stuff and appeared real pale, especially when everyone else in the room had a tan. I just couldn't imagine how this woman could have beat Mike when he was younger.

I sat on the davenport beside Shelia who sort of played with my hands and head like I was her toy. I didn't know how to get out of it.

"Leave off 'im," Charley blurted at Shelia. "Whaterya tryin to do, get him...."

"Hey! Charley," Mike broke in. "Tommy's eight, don't forget."

"So whatdaya want from me? I don't know from kids. I only was one once and when I was one I was always thinking..."

"Stop!" Shelia clamped her hand over Charley's mouth. Everyone laughed, even me, although I didn't know what he meant.

It went on like this for a long time. Whatever anyone mentioned, it turned into an argument: *President Truman, Manhattan and Brooklyn* (where Charley was from), *baseball*, "You hear about that nigger playing in Jersey City last year? Robinson?" "Well, hell, Hank Greenberg played for the Tigers so it's just a matter of time you ask me."

I didn't know about Hank Greenberg but I knew that "nigger" was a bad word. I looked around the room but no one, including Mike, seemed bothered.

"Sid Gordon, plays for the Giants. He's a kike." Charley allowed.

"Hey Combat!" Mike yelled. "Just one damned minute here. Tommy's Jewish. Let's show a little respect, you don't mind."

"You kiddin' me?" Charley said, looking a little annoyed at Mike. "A yid at the Murphy's Sunday dinner. Who woulda thought?"

"Okay, all a youse," Mrs. Murphy called from the kitchen. "See if you can shut your mouths so that nothin' comes out and only food goes in. Dinner is served!"

I was beginning to feel what Mike had been telling me about, but so far most of it was coming from Charley and Mike didn't grow up with him.

When we were seated and Mrs. Murphy had put all the food on the table, Shelia asked, "We gonna say grace?"

"We never say grace," Mike snapped at her.

"Well, I just thought, with Tommy here and all, we should show some respect to our Father."

"You're a little trouble-maker, that's what," Mike snarled at her.

"Stop it, you two," Mrs. Murphy yelled. Then she smiled at me and passed a bowl of mashed potatoes.

"You allowed to eat ham, Tommy?" Mr. Murphy wanted to know.

"Sure," I said. "Why not?"

He laughed. "You know: 'Hoiby, Heimy, Maxie, Sam. They're the boys that won't eat ham."

I looked at him waiting for more, so I could understand what he was asking me. He just laughed.

Mike got really mad and raised his voice. "Will you guys stop it already?"

"Stop what?" his father asked.

"All this anti-Semitic stuff. You know, we fought a war so we could have some peace in the world. Could we just please have a little at this table, today? Please?"

Everyone stopped talking, took food, passed the dishes around and began eating. No talking. Just knives on plates and forks against teeth and water slurping. Mike's father drank beer from a bottle. When the food came to me, Mike served me and spoke softly, asking me what I wanted and how much. I was beginning to feel like I did when I went to my grandparents in the Bronx. Except for Mike and his mom.

"Tommy!" Mrs. Murphy called from the kitchen when we'd finished eating and Shelia had cleared the table. "You by any chance like cherry pie with chocolate ice cream on top?"

"My favorite!"

We ate and the adults drank coffee and talked to each other. It was okay.

Then, Mike's father asked me, "So, Tommy, I hear your dad was shot down at Midway, piloting a B-26. That's really tough."

"Kevin!" Mrs. Murphy yelled from the kitchen. "Leave him alone. I'm sure he don't like to talk about it." She toweled her hands and came back to the table. It was like she was guarding me.

"That's service men, Ma." Shelia said. "Not kids."

I didn't say anything. No one had asked me a question and I knew Mike hadn't told them any of the things I had said to him.

"So whadaya say, kid?" Mr. Murphy questioned. "You proud of your old man, givin' his life for his country?"

"Yeah, I'm proud of him for that." I swallowed hard. "But I miss him. I wish he didn't have to die. I wish no one had to die in wars." Mike squeezed my knee under the table.

"You can blame the krauts and the Japs for that, sonny," Charley put in. "The fuckin', er, ah, sorry. It just makes me mad, that's all."

"Why you so mad?" Mr. Murphy wanted to know. "You wasn't anywhere near the war." He looked at me. "Charley, here, was not drafted because he was in a 'critical industry'—ladies undergarments." Everyone laughed except Charley.

"Don't laugh. If we didn't do what we did maybe it woulda been your wife, mother or sister whose elastic waist band snapped and she lost her drawers in the middle of Broadway." The adults screamed with laughter.

Shelia said, "That actually happened to my girlfriend. And crossing Broadway too. Downtown. Panties fell right to her ankles."

I thought they were all going to choke from laughing. I didn't really get it, although it did seem funny thinking of a girl's underpants falling off.

"What'd she do?" Mrs. Murphy asked.

"She just stepped out of them and kept walking, like they wasn't hers." More hoots and howls

"Jeez!" said Charley. "I sure woulda like to find 'em."

No one laughed.

"Tommy," Shelia said. "I bet you didn't know Mike was a war hero. A decorated hero. Distinguished Flying Cross."

I thought I felt Mike tighten into a corkscrew. He said, "Shut up, Shelia. I mean it."

"See," she sneered. "The guys in combat won't talk about it. I don't know why. I'm proud my little brother was a bombardier in a B-29." She got up from the table. "Ma. Where's the scrapbook? Let's show Tommy."

"No!" Mike screamed at her.

Something was very wrong in that room but I didn't know what it was. I began to get pretty scared, thinking there was going to be a fist fight. I tried to remember where the subway stop was.

Shelia ignored him and went into a room off the dining room.

Mr. Murphy was saying, "Most guys are proud to be in on making the Japs surrender. Not my son. He wants to hide it."

"Hey, Mikey!" Charley yelled. "I didn't know you was no hero. Get out! Whadaya, modest? After what those little nips did wherever they went? You ever hear the stories about how they raped a million girls in Australia? And they was white, too."

Mrs. Murphy looked disgusted. "It was Nanking in China, not Australia. The women were Chinese, not white. And it was twenty-thousand not a million, though one is too many. You ignoramus. Shelia!" she called into the next room. "You not thinking of marrying this ape are ya? We may not be the smartest family, but we got more brains than this cockroach." Charley slumped back in his chair.

Mike had left the table and was standing by the window, staring across the fire escape out into the South Bronx. He looked very upset.

"I got it!" Shelia yelled and came running back into the dining room and slammed a scrapbook down on the table in front of me, sitting in Mike's chair and pulling it close to me. She flipped open the cover and then to the last page when Mike reached her and tried to grab the book from her. She was ready and snapped it away, got up, knocking over her chair, and turned and ran to the other side of the table.

She read: "Airman First Class Michael Murphy of New York, New York...." Mike ran at her and she dashed to the other side of the table. Everyone but me was standing up, just watching, like no one knew what to do. I didn't know what was happening.

"Shelia!" Mike yelled, really loud. "Gimme that! It's mine!"

"Matter of fact," Mrs. Murphy said, "It's mine. I kept it for you."

"...awarded the Distinguished Flying Cross for extraordinary bravery in the face of enemy anti-aircraft fire...."

Mike ran around the table and lunged at her but she was too quick for him.

"...in a low-flying B-29...."

"Shelia! Please! Don't read it. Please!" Mike had stopped chasing her and had fallen into the chair beside his mother and next to me. He looked terrified.

"...was one of the bombardiers that dropped incendiary ordinance on the civilian population of Tokyo." Her voice dropped. "I never read this before," she said. "Seventeen hundred tons of bombs were dropped on densely populated areas, causing fire storms that killed 130,000 civilians, most of them women and children....' "Michael." She dropped the book on the table, crossed her arms in front of her, put her face in her folded arms and sobbed.

Mike had fallen to the floor at his mother's knees and had buried his own face in her lap, crying and crying like a child. "I'm sorry, everyone. I didn't mean to burn up anyone, especially children. We flew so low we could see their faces. Everything burning! Burning!"

Mike's mother patted his head and gazed down at him, her face tight-lipped and ashamed, not sad and sympathetic like my mom's was when I needed her. Mr. Murphy had gone into the living room and turned on the radio and was spinning the dial looking for something. Charley got up, walked to the apartment door, looked back in disgust at the entire family and left.

I waited a little while then quietly left too. Mom always had me carry a five dollar bill just in case. I remembered where the subway entrance was and walked up the steep hill from Mike's building, his secret hotter in my memory than the blazing three o'clock August, New York sun.

CHAPTER 8

After leaving Mike's, I had trouble making it up Hilltop Hill or whatever its name was. I couldn't stop thinking of him crying in his mother's lap and begging to be forgiven. I was pretty sure that what he did, along with a lot of other bombardiers, was drop firebombs (I'd seen about them in the Newsreel) on Tokyo. And their planes flew so low—how was that even possible for a B-29?—that he could actually see the faces of the little kids burning up. Whew! That made me sick. No wonder it made him crazy and ashamed and he wanted to keep it secret. And boy! What a terrible family. They were so ugly how they acted, especially to Mike on the bombs.

As I plugged along, getting hotter and hotter and sweaty all over, the people and cars and streets and buildings looked different than before. They all seemed horrible and smelly, as if the world was rotting and I hadn't noticed it just a few hours ago. Not one person was smiling or laughing, none of the cars were clean, and a lot of trash lay against the curbs and on the sidewalk. The buildings and street poles and traffic lights and signs were dirty and looked as if they would fall down any minute. When I got to Broadway, all the store windows were gray and streaked and the things showing in them appeared limp and awful; I couldn't see how anyone would want to buy them.

By the time I got to the train, tears were rolling down my cheeks and I felt like one of those kids who had been burned up. Even if they were Japs, that was bad. But I couldn't get Mike inside that word. It was as if he'd been forced to go in that B-29 and drop those bombs or else get shot or maybe thrown out of the plane. He seemed so sorry for what he'd done. Was my daddy sorry for what he'd done in the war? Was everyone who killed someone in wars sorry afterwards?

The minute I got in the door I ran to Mom and fell into her arms and started bawling. Susan was there too and after I told them what had happened, I guess she felt sorry for me because she came over and knelt down beside me and stroked the back of my head and shoulders.

Mom finally said, "I understand now why Mike seems a little child-like: he had his innocence ripped out of him. How could the United States do such a thing? I knew it happened but not the number dead. That's more than either the Hiroshima or Nagasaki atomic bombs killed."

She and Susan began to cry so I started again.

I asked, "Was Daddy sorry that he killed people?"

"I don't know if he ever did. Midway was pretty early in the war and I don't think he was in any other battles. I don't know the answer to your question, Tommy. Men fight in wars and not very many of them talk about what happened. I think that's because it's too awful and doesn't fit into any of the ways men live their civilian lives."

"What about women?" Susan asked. "You think we'd be different?"

"You bet I do! I can't see any woman dropping bombs on people and killing a lot of other human beings with machine guns. Would you do it?"

"Gad no!"

"The world would be a different place if women ran it, believe me."

I didn't understand them, as usual. When Susan beat me up when Mom wasn't around she didn't seem any different than a brother would be.

After Susan went to make phone calls, I said to Mom, "The thing is, I know what Mike means; how he feels."

"What?" Mom said. "What on earth are you talking about?"

"He thinks he did something bad by killing those children. With fire. And I...." I hesitated, not sure how to say what I wanted. She waited. "I think Daddy can't be dead 'til I find him. That, after the explosion and the fire, he died but some part of him needs to be found, seen, touched by me before he can be all dead. Forever. And I'm bad because I haven't found him. Mike's trying to let all those kids be all dead too, but he doesn't know how. Like me."

"Well, well, Mr. Sartre himself! You've got it partly right."

"What?"

"Tommy, Tommy. What am I going to do with you? How can I get through to you?" She came and sat beside me on the davenport and put her arm around me and pulled me to her. "Daddy's gone. Those children are gone. Six million Jews are gone. Nothing can bring them back. Neither you nor Mike have any special powers. What both of you must do is stop thinking about the dead and focus on everything that's alive, especially yourselves. You understand?"

"I don't feel that. Isn't it possible that I'm right?"

"No!" She slapped both hands on her knees and frowned. Her cheeks pinkended. It was like she was teaching me not to run into the streets.

"How can you be so sure?"

She threw her hands in the air and stood. "I give up. You're stubborn just like your father." She turned to leave but stopped and looked back to me. "But you also have that wonderful Jewish quality, the tradition of the Talmudic rabbis of questioning everything, of accepting nothing as final." She smiled and gave me a hug.

It didn't help.

***

Mike wouldn't be my friend anymore after that day. I went to the firehouse a couple of times but the men said Mike was too busy to come out. I got it. I knew his secret and he couldn't look at me anymore. I wished so much that I could get him to know it didn't mean anything bad to me; that I would always be his friend.

63

I sure felt sad all the time. I took my glove and ball and told Mom I was going to play ball but I just walked up and down the streets of the neighborhood. I even walked along Columbus, never feeling any danger. Once, a kid came up to me, pushed me down and stole my glove. The ball rolled into the street. He ran, but right away a bigger kid grabbed him by his shirt and snatched my glove.

"Leave 'im alone, Johnny. He's a friend a Fireman Mike." He tossed the glove back to me. "Stay offa Columbus, Jew boy. I ain't always gonna be around." All of that and I still only felt sad.

Everyone saw it and worried: Mom, Susan, my friends (their mothers called mine), and when school started, my teacher wrote a note home. I started having bad dreams, always sorta the same. There was some kind of trouble and I got scared that something bad was going to happen to me. I ran toward help, but the person or people always ran away from me. I woke up crying a lot of times. Mom was quick to come to my bedside to comfort me.

***

Finally, I just couldn't take it anymore. I decided to make Mike talk to me, to listen to me. If I could only tell him that nothing he'd done made any difference to me—Mom was right about that—he'd be my friend again. And I could stop being sad. Yet I knew that Mike wasn't the whole of it.

On Saturday night after dinner and cleaning up I told Mom I was going to play with Henry and the guys. It was still light out.

64

"Be back by nine," she said, not looking up from her book.

I ran down to 83rd Street and up to the firehouse. The lights were all on, the garage door was open and the fire truck was gone. My heart squeezed. A fire! Mike had gone to a fire. He had told me they'd gone on a couple of calls in the weeks since he'd met me, but nothing big. I just knew this was big.

Duffy was there—Mike had said they always had more than a full crew at the station in case something happened to one guy; he got sick or something.

"Hi, Duffy. Where's Mike?"

"Hiya, kiddo. Out on a call. This is a big one. Four alarm. Didn't you hear the sirens?"

"Er, ah, sure," I lied. I didn't hear anything these days, even on the streets of New York. "Where is it?"

"Eighty-eighth between Amsterdam and Columbus. Right around the corner from you. You could probably watch it from your apartment window."

"We look out on 86th Street." I didn't even say goodbye; just ran as fast as I could toward the fire. Toward Mike.

When I got to 88th Street, the cops had an empty car blocking the street. I could see the burning brownstone half way up the block. It looked like five or six fire engines were there. Fire blew out of some of the building's windows and the almost night sky was black with smoke.

65

I started to walk up the sidewalk and a cop grabbed me.

"Stay back, sonny."

"I live on this block. At 148. My mom will be really worried if I don't get home. You know, with the fire and all."

He looked at me, apparently deciding I was not capable of such a lie and let me pass. I ran as fast as I could toward the fire. I spotted the Engine Co. 74 truck and rushed up to it. The whole street was like a war battlefield: hoses all over the place, water running down the gutters, two ambulances, firemen, cops, ambulance guys and people everywhere. One guy was taking pictures with a big camera and flashbulbs. The red and white lights on the fire trucks, cop cars and ambulances turned and blinked. A lot of people were yelling: instructions, curses, calls for equipment or water, names, and a few women were screaming and crying. There were people trapped in the building. Big fire hoses sprayed huge water spurts at the windows and three hoses ran from fire trucks up the stairs and into the brownstone.

I looked for Mike everywhere. I just had to see him okay with my own eyes. I had a terrible feeling, a waking dream of his face burned up like the children he'd firebombed.

"Mike! Mike! Mike Murphy!" I called as loud as I could. No one answered. I ran all around looking into the face of every fireman I came on. I couldn't even find anyone from Mike's firehouse.

Two firemen ran out the front door and down the stairs with people over their shoulders. They raced to the ambulances and flopped the people over onto stretchers on the ground. I saw one lady who looked burned up like a black marshmallow. She smelled horrible. An ambulance guy bent over her, touched her neck, shook his head and said something to another guy in white. That man got a black blanket out of the back of the ambulance and covered her with it. Gosh! She was dead! Was she all dead? Was anyone all dead? Ever? Or was it only Daddy and the Jap kids?

I began to feel dizzy and my heart was beating so fast it felt like Gene Krupa was drumming in my chest.

"Tommy! What're you doing here?" It was Sean from the 74th.

"I'm looking for Mike. Where is he?" My words shook as they spurted out.

"He's inside. With a bunch of other guys. There's still people in there. We can hear 'em. Even some kids." He put his sooty hand up to his smoke smeared face and sobbed. "It's terrible. A terrible fire. The worst I ever seen. Jesus and Mary!" He turned away.

I looked to the burning building. Flames flew out of a bunch of windows. The tall ladders on both sides of the stoop up to the fourth floor were empty. I could see that no one could climb them and get close to those windows. Mike was inside. Burning up. I knew like I knew my name that he was after the kids and wouldn't come out till he'd gotten them all. Or died trying.

Boom! Boom! Pieces of the building and glass blew out of one of the windows. I ducked. A big ball of fire followed and I could feel everything throb and shake.

"Backdraft!" a fireman said.

"Mike!" I screamed. A huge arm crossed my chest, lifted me off the ground and carried me away. Sean had me across his hip. "Mike! Mike! No! Let me go! I gotta find him! Let me go!" I kicked my legs. He set me down and wrapped me in both arms. Boom! Another blast.

"No one's comin' outa that place alive," Sean moaned. "Mosta the crew's in there." Tears from his blood-shot eyes watered his blackened cheeks. He just kept shaking his head and squeezing me and crying.

"Tommy! Oh, thank God! I knew you'd be here."

"Mom!" Her and my voices sounded so far away and she looked tiny in front of me. Everything did, like I was looking through a peephole on the inside of an apartment door.

She gathered me in her arms and sunk down on the street behind the wheel of a fire truck. Right in the water. My teeth began to chatter and Sean took his coat off and laid it over me. One of the ambulance guys came out of the smoke towards me, a tiny little man like one of my toys. I closed my eyes and don't remember anything more.

CHAPTER 9

I dreamed that Mike was by my bed, all sooty and bloody, but alive. Mom was there too, standing beside him, smiling, looking down at me. Susan was behind her. Mike's and Mom's lips moved but no sound came out. They smiled and put their hands out to touch me but I couldn't feel anything. They looked regular sized.

Mike knelt and talked to me. No sound. He was dead. *Dead Men Don't Talk*. The *Marvel Mystery Comics* cover floated by the back of my eyes.

Susan disappeared, then came back and gave Mom something. Mom's hands moved round and round till she reached them toward my face and laid something across my forehead. I didn't feel anything. Maybe I was dead. Everyone dead. All dead? All gone? The marshmallow woman? The 83rd Street fire station crew? The children in the burning building? All gone dead?

Daddy wasn't there. Mike was there. Where was Daddy? Up in the sky. Dead Daddy up in the sky but not all dead. Tommy will make him all dead.

The dream was over and everyone was gone. I got out of my bed into a darkened room. I could feel again but my whole body had turned into my heart

69

and it was shattered like the building glass because Mike was dead. Fireman Mike died trying to save burning children. I fell to my knees, buried my face back into my sheets and cried a little.

I sniffed my tears away. I didn't have time to cry now. I put on my underpants, dungarees, shirt, and socks and shoes and crept out of my room. I knew Mom and Susan were alive and asleep and if they heard me they wouldn't let me go find Daddy. I had to go. I had to do this and be done so I could be a regular kid again and stop crying all the time. My heart was aching two ways: for all the dead who kept becoming important to me, and for my vanishing boyhood.

I slipped down the hallway and out the front door. Maybe I could find Mike and Daddy.

I opened the door to the stairs and began walking up to the roof of my building, the 13th floor. The apartments ended on the 12th and so did the elevator, but I always said that my building had thirteen floors.

Stepping out onto the tar paper right away I could smell smoke; lots of it. The building. I went to the uptown wall and hoisted myself up. Sure enough there was 88th Street and the glow and smoke of the burning building. I fell off my perch and crumpled to the roof top, huddled against the wall and began drowning in a flood of tears for Mike. The best friend I ever had. What would I do without him?

I must have cried myself to sleep, because when I woke up it was light out. The sun was well up on the East River side. Then I realized I must have been asleep a long time down in my bed, earlier. It had been way before nine o'clock when I had gone to the fire. A lot of sleep but I was still so tired all over my body.

I remembered why I'd come up to the roof and stood. I didn't want to look toward the building where Mike had died. It would make me too sad again and I wouldn't be able to do what I had to do. I wished I could fly like Superman; all the way to Krypton. Just for an hour or two. That would settle everything.

So I dragged over to the water tower and took hold of the lowest ladder rung and began my final journey to find my father and help him become all the way dead.

It was easy for the first few rungs, but then, for some reason it got harder. I felt tired but not scared. I was still on the part of the ladder below the bottom of the water tower.

When I got to the base things changed. I could see out into the neighborhood. I held on to the sides of the metal ladder, grimy with rust, and tried to identify places. The Belnord across Amsterdam was as high as our building. Kitty-cornered was a kid from my school's building. It was twenty stories so blocked a lot of downtown and the Hudson River.

I climbed higher, along the side of the water tower. The rungs were closer to the wooden side of the tower so I couldn't put my whole foot on. Up I went, rung-by-rung, just keeping my eyes on the wood shingles in front of me.

The higher I got the closer to Daddy I felt I was getting. I just knew I'd find the hole in the sky and see him; maybe touch him.

Suddenly, a wind blew on me. Not really a wind like on a windy day. More like going to the top of a hill and feeling the air moving faster than on the ground. A breeze Mom would call it. But it was quick-moving and startled me and I squeezed the ladder sides tighter. As I climbed, the breeze seemed to pick up speed and move around in little bursts, first from one side and then another; from the top then the bottom. Maybe this was the air moving an opening in the sky for me to look through.

When I got to the roof of the water tower the ladder angled up over the lip and went on to the very top. There were only eight or nine more rungs along the cone. I could see a block of wood with a metal handle just down from the top, to the side of the ladder. That must be why the ladder went all the way up; so workmen could open the little door and maybe even climb down into the tower and fix something.

I didn't care. I just wanted to get to the top. It was hard getting over the bend and I wondered about getting back down. I wasn't afraid of the height. I thought I would be, but I kept trying to remember climbing to the top of our tree back in Hutchinson. Still, I wouldn't look at anything except the wood and the ladder rungs. The breeze became more of a wind and started to scare me a little.

Finally, my hand reached the last rung and I stopped. I held on tight. I didn't really want to look into the sky. I was afraid to see Daddy now that I was so close. I thought about him in his B-26, up in the sky like me, looking down over all the ships and the Pacific Ocean. Then, BOOM! He was burning. Like Mike's children. Like Mike. Dead, but something left. Not all dead.

I took a deep breath and looked up into the sky. It was bright now and I couldn't look east because the sun was there. Blue sky. The water tower in front of me and blue sky above and around me. I even took a chance and looked behind me. Blue sky. No hole. No Daddy. No Mike. Just blue sky and New York City. Down at 72nd Street, Amsterdam crossed Broadway. A big "X." Like "No!" or "Wrong!" There was no hole. There never had been a hole. Daddy wasn't there. He wasn't floating in the sky waiting for me to make him all dead, he was already all dead. He was all dead at Midway.

I started to cry. How could I have been so dumb? How could I never see him again? I felt so alone and lonely. Mom and Susan weren't enough. My friends weren't enough. Mike had been almost enough. Everyone leaves. There was just me. I cried more and felt weak. My hands weren't holding tight enough.

I looked out over New York, realizing just how high up I was; and I wasn't inside or on a roof's floor. The back of my legs hurt and my stomach began to roll and my head got lighter and lighter. For the first time in my life I was afraid of a high place. Really afraid. And I was on a very, very high place. Stupid. And for nothing. All of a sudden I didn't think I could get down. I didn't want to look down and even when I looked at the City it made me afraid because I was so high. So I just clung to the ladder and put my face against the wood between two rungs and wet it with my tears.

My hands were sweaty. They had been dry before. My heart was pounding, my legs started feeling wobbly and I was getting dizzy. Maybe this was the meaning of the hole in the sky and finding Daddy: I was going to fall off and get killed and be with Daddy. I tried to go down but I was so scared my feet wouldn't move. I just wanted to be down not climb down. The more I wanted to be down the more afraid I got. It felt like my whole everything was going red and black with fear. I cried. I sweat all over. I got faint. I began to slip.

I heard and felt something at the same moment: a voice and arms around me and a body pressed against my back.

"Don't move, Tommy."

It was Mike's voice. Now I knew I had already fallen and was dead with him. But I could feel him. He was warm on me. Then I saw his hands gripping the ladder rung just above mine.

"Take a step down one rung, buddy. Don't be afraid. You can't fall. I've got you pressed in. You're totally safe."

I did as he said, not understanding whether I was alive or dead. Not understanding how he could be there. Had he come from the dead to save me?

None of that. Once we were down, he hauled me into the stairwell and sat me down on the top step, pulling me against him, his arm around my body.

I was wracked with fear and trembles and sobs. I was so sick of crying.

"How...." I whispered.

"I grabbed the two kids from the building and got out the back. Before the explosions. We all did. The 74th is whole."

I was glad but didn't feel much of it. I was going numb again. I guess he could see it because he pinched the skin on my arm really hard.

"Stay with me buddy-boy. You don't remember my coming to see you in your apartment by your bed?"

"See me? I thought that was a dream."

"Nah. You were in a little shock. Seen it many times around fires. I thought so but didn't know you couldn't get that I was alive. Must a been horrible for you."

I looked up into his face, pouted and nodded my head. He would never know how hard it had been.

"When your mom saw you'd left the apartment, she got scared and called me. I knew just where you'd gone. And why." He waited and I snuggled against him a little more. I was safe and he was alive.

"So, did you find your dad up there? Any hole in the sky?"

"No. Just sky. I feel so dumb thinking all that junk. And actually climbing that monster out there.... I don't know. Whadayou think about the whole thing? Did you see that dead woman at the fire? I couldn't stop thinking of you seeing that on all the children in Tokyo. You know?"

"Yeah, I know. I seen her. I've seen plenty of dead people at fires. And the kids, like you say. I been thinkin' a lot since you was up for dinner and I'm pretty sure I figured the whole thing out."

"What's the answer?"

"Nothing."

"What?"

"There's nothing after death, just whatever living people remember of the dead ones. No heaven, no nothing."

"So where's my Daddy?"

"In your heart big guy. But him as a body and mind and whatever else is in people is all gone."

A strange quiet crept over me from his words and ideas, like warm water washing away a lot of stuff stuck to me from rolling around wrestling. I felt calm. Convinced. Okay with "nothing."

I stretched, felt hungry and said, "Let's get breakfast and go behind the fire house and have a catch."

"Now you're talkin.' But first we gotta go see your mom. She's very worried about you. That's something."

ABOUT THE AUTHOR

Idrian Resnick was born in Wichita, Kansas and raised on the Upper West Side in Manhattan. He has spent his career as a writer, innovator, advocate, and educator. With a Ph.D. in economics and African Studies from Boston University, Resnick taught there and at Howard, Princeton, Columbia, Cornell and the University of Dar es Salaam in Tanzania, where, later, he served as an adviser to the government. He founded and directed the Economic Development Bureau, a progressive non-profit economic and financial consulting organization for Global South countries. Resnick served as the Executive Director of the Association on American Indian Affairs, and directed Action for Corporate Accountability, which led the boycott against Nestle for its unethical promotion of infant formula. In the course of his career, he has traveled to, lived and worked in some fifty-five countries. He lives with his wife in Branford, Connecticut.